This book belongs to ....

To Tricia, Mike, Yasmin and Natasha
– with love

A Bantam Little Rooster Book/October 1989

All rights reserved.

Copyright © 1989 by Simon James.

Originally published by J. M. Dent & Sons Ltd., London.

Little Rooster is a trademark of Bantam Books, a division
of Bantam Doubleday Dell Publishing Group, Inc.

Library of Congress Cataloging-in-Publication Data:

James, Simon.
    The day Jake vacuumed.

    "A Bantam little rooster book."
    "Originally published by J.M. Dent & Sons Ltd., London"—T.p. verso.
    Summary: Jake, who does not like helping people or having others tell him
what to do, signals his displeasure at being asked to vacuum by sucking his
entire family into the vacuum cleaner.
    [1. Vacuum cleaners—Fiction. 2. Behavior—Fiction] I. Title.
PZ7.J1544 Day 1989 [E] 88-36034
ISBN 0-553-05840-1

The Day Jake
Vacuumed

Simon James

A BANTAM LITTLE ROOSTER BOOK
TORONTO · NEW YORK · LONDON · SYDNEY · AUCKLAND

Jake was difficult.
Jake was a problem.
He didn't like doing
anything for anyone.

So you can imagine how Jake felt the day his mother asked him to do the vacuum cleaning. For a while, Jake played with the machine, enjoying the loud noise it made.

Then he got a truly nasty idea. Very quietly, he crept over to Timmy. Aiming the nozzle, Jake switched on the vacuum... and sucked up the poor cat!

Jake was delighted. He knew he would be in trouble, though. "If I'm going to be in trouble," he thought, "I might as well be in BIG TROUBLE!"
So off he sneaked to the kitchen...

. . . and sucked his mother up into the vacuum cleaner, rubber gloves and all!

"I'm free!" shouted Jake. "No one to tell me
what to do." He had the whole house to
himself except, that is, for his icky little sister,

who was in her bedroom playing with her dolls.
In crept Jake.
And with a flip of the switch, up she went.
The dolls went, too.

Jake wondered what his father would say
when he came home.
There was only one thing to do.

At six o'clock on the dot, his father opened
the front door. Out jumped Jake with the
vacuum cleaner roaring on full power.
It was a tight squeeze at first, but
eventually... Jake's father went in
with a *POP!*

"Hooray!" shouted Jake.
He was in charge at last. Jake was so
pleased with himself that he decided to
suck up the *whole* room, and...

. . . most of this book. That left Jake and
the vacuum cleaner – and nothing but
white space everywhere.

After two hours of total freedom, Jake was
beginning to get restless. He didn't notice
that the vacuum cleaner had started to
shake and rattle. In fact, it sounded as
though it might even...

EXPLODE!!! With a gigantic bang, out flew the family –
every which way! Once Jake's parents recovered, they were furious.
They sent him to bed without any supper.

But Jake wasn't too upset. At least he knew he would never ever be asked to do the vacuuming again.